PLAGUE

The apothecary examined my father's eyes closely. He sniffed around his mouth. My father's chest was covered with dark marks, like bruises.

'Alas, Mistress Harper, it is plague. Not all patients have the buboes. Some have dark marks on the skin. Madam, you must prepare yourself. Your husband is dying.'

SHARP SHADES

PLAGUE

Look out for other exciting stories
in the *Sharp Shades* series:

A Murder of Crows by Penny Bates
Shouting at the Stars by David Belbin
Witness by Anne Cassidy
Doing the Double by Alan Durant
Tears of a Friend by Joanna Kenrick
Blitz by David Orme
Hunter's Moon by John Townsend

SHARP SHADES

PLAGUE

By David Orme
Adapted by David Belbin

Evans

Published by Evans Brothers Limited
2A Portman Mansions
Chiltern St
London W1U 6NR

British Library Cataloguing in Publication Data
Orme, David
    Plague. - Differentiated ed. - (Sharp shades)
    1. Plague - England - London - History - 17th
    century -
    Fiction 2. London (England) - History - 17th
    century -
    Fiction 3. Historical fiction 4. Young adult
    fiction
    I. Title
    823.9'14[J]

ISBN-13: 9780237535223

Series Editor: David Belbin
Editor: Julia Moffatt
Designer: Rob Walster
Picture research: Bryony Jones

This abridged edition was first published in its
original form as a *Shades* title of the same name.

Picture acknowledgements:
istockphoto.com: pp 15, 18, 21, 26, 33, 36, 51 and
55. Bryony Jones: pp 8 and 40

Contents

Chapter One
Struck Down

'The plague is running through the city,' Master Coulter told his wife. 'Five new cases in Newgate Street. Tomorrow you must go to the country with Mary.'

I had been apprentice to John Coulter for six months. I wanted to be an apothecary, like him.

Master Coulter looked at me.

'And what of you, lad? Will you stay with me, or will you return to your family? I'll not stand in your way.'

There came a loud knocking at the door. Mistress Coulter sent Mary to answer it.

'Whoever it is, send them away. Your master can do no more today.'

But it was my older brother, Jasper.

'I am sorry to come to you so late,'

he said. 'Father has been struck down. I beg you, sir, could you attend on him?'

'Come along, Henry,' my master said. 'Your father is a good man. Let us see what ails him.'

My father's shop was a short distance away. Cheapside was busy. People were filling carts with all they owned.

'Fear of the plague is spreading fast,' said Master Coulter.

'Do you fear the plague, Master Coulter?' asked Jasper. 'You are in contact with the sick every day.'

'I fear it, but not for myself. When

I was young, I was struck down with plague. But I recovered. You cannot catch the plague a second time. Why that is, I do not know.'

We reached my father's shop. My mother was at the door.

'Master Coulter, thank the Lord you are here!'

Upstairs, my father lay groaning and coughing. His face was dead white and lined with pain. He coughed blood.

'It can't be plague,' my mother said. 'Look, there is no sign of the buboes upon him. Please, tell me sir, it is not plague!'

The apothecary examined my father's eyes closely. He sniffed around his mouth. My father's chest was covered with dark marks, like bruises.

'Alas, Mistress Harper, it is plague. Not all patients have the buboes. Some have dark marks on the skin. Madam, you must prepare yourself. Your husband is dying.'

Chapter Two
Attack in the Night

Jasper did his best to comfort our mother.

I asked, 'Is there nothing you can do?'

'Nothing, lad,' the apothecary said.

'What of the potion you gave to Sir William Hunter yesterday?'

'Some potions make the patient feel better. They swell my purse a little. That's all.'

My mother grabbed his hand.

'Sir, we'll try anything.'

'You may try it if you wish,'

Master Coulter said. 'I have none about me. Henry will return with it. Your husband should drink it down, if he is able.'

I was unwilling to leave my family. But I had to. It was so busy the short journey took a long time. Master Coulter was tired out when we reached his house. His wife made him eat and rest before he made the potion. It was nearly midnight before I set out for Aldersgate Street. It was dark in the busy streets. I made my way home by a back way through the dark alleys. As a result, I soon became lost.

'Who be this then?'

I turned to run but there was someone else behind me. Blows rained down on my poor body until I could feel them no more.

I opened my eyes. I put my hand in my pocket, but it was empty. Master Coulter's potion had gone. In pain, I set off to Aldersgate Street.

There must have been many more plague cases overnight. Houses were shut up. Watchmen stood outside. They let no one out. Ugly red crosses were painted on the doors. I reached my father's shop. The door was unlocked. I pushed it open and went in. All was silent and still. My mother and brother were gone. In the tiny bedroom, my poor father lay dead.

Chapter Three
Searchers and Watchmen

I found a note on the table downstairs. It told me my mother and brother had gone to my uncle's farm. They had left money in a jug for my father's funeral. I was to follow them if I was able.

For a moment, I was angry with my mother and brother for leaving without me. But when I thought about it, I knew they were right to go. I took the money from the jug and hurried to our family church. It was crowded with people reporting deaths. At last I reached the desk.

'Henry Harper, isn't it?' the parish clerk said. 'So your father is dead. He was a fine man, Henry, and these are sad times. Return to your home lad, and wait for the searchers. Put a shroud upon your father. He will be collected at nightfall.'

'Where will his grave be?'

'Henry, look in the churchyard!
See what we have come to!'

Men were digging a deep pit.
Next to it was another pit. Corpses
were laid out head to toe. The
gravediggers were too busy to cover
them with soil before they put more
corpses on top.

Noon came. A woman banged on
the door.

'Where is it?' she asked.

'Where is what?'

'The body, boy. I'm the parish
searcher. I needs to see what he
died of.'

'For what purpose?'

'The bills, boy.'

I had forgotten the bills of mortality. Our parish clerk had to list the cause of death. The old woman peered at the cold corpse. She sniffed at it just as Master Coulter had done. Then she went to the window.

'Barney! Plague!'

She returned to the street without a further word.

My duty was with Master Coulter. I had work to do. So I went down to the street and pushed open the door.

'Oi! You lad! Get back in there!'

It was Barney, a rough man who cleaned the parish gutters.

'Who says I must? Get out of my way!'

'The parish says you must, and I'm watchman for these houses. You stay there on pain of death!'

I went back into the house.

'But how long must I remain here?'

'Until it's your turn for the dead-cart.'

He thought I had the plague too! Another neighbour came to the house. This was Thomas Jenkins, a family friend. I called to him.

'Mr Jenkins! Please, tell them that I cannot remain here!'

But Mr Jenkins carried a pot of red paint. He ignored me and painted a cross on the front door.

Chapter Four
The Plague Pit

All our friends had turned against me. Later, I understood. They were afraid and had to protect their own families.

My first duty was to my father. I

knew my mother kept shrouds for Father and herself. I found them at the bottom of the chest in the bedroom. I took off the clothes my father was wearing. I gave them a good shake out of the window. They were full of fleas. Barney stood below. He got covered. Fleas are harmless, but at least they made my jailer itch.

Night came, and it began to rain. Soon, I heard Barney going off duty. Another man replaced him. Half an hour later, I heard the clatter of iron wheels. A voice called out.

'Dead! Dead! Bring out your dead!'

I looked out. Stiff corpses were pushed out of doors and windows by the families inside. Other houses were dark. The dead-cart men broke the doors down if they were locked. Then they brought out the bodies.

I thought of a way to escape. But could I make it work?

I found my mother's shroud and wrapped it round myself. It was a struggle, but I managed. By the time the cart was outside my house I was next to my father on the bed. The body collector spoke to the new watchman.

'How many in here, Tommy?'

'Don't know. Only just got here.'

I heard the door opening below, and the sound of boots on the stairs.

'Two.'

They took my father first, then came back for me.

'This one's still warm. Can't have been dead long.'

Luckily for me, both men were drunk and stupid. They should have wondered how the one who died last could wrap himself in his own shroud. I was carried out into the street and thrown into the cart. There were many more bodies to collect in the parish. It was hard to

breathe with all the corpses on top
of me. Some had been dead for days.
The weather had been warm, and
their smell was terrible.

I felt the cart bounce over the
rough ground of the graveyard. One
by one, the corpses were dropped
into the pit. Luckily, the pit was
almost full. A fall into an empty one
could have killed me.

Time passed. I hoped the cart had
gone off to collect more corpses. I
had to get myself out of the pit. This
was difficult. The shroud was tight. I
managed to kick my legs free. I
pushed my way up a little. Luckily,

there were only two layers of corpses on top of me. When I reached the top of the heap, I took the shroud off. The edge of the pit was only four feet above me. It was now full of bodies. They would soon be covered with quick-lime and earth. I was lucky to have time to escape.

There was no one in the graveyard. I crossed the damp ground and slipped through the gate into Aldersgate Street. I was free, but where should I go?

Chapter Five
Into the City

I had to try and reach my mother
and brother. My uncle's farm was in
Camberwell, south of the river. I had
no money for the boat. It had to be
London Bridge. I was lightly dressed.

Luckily, the rain had stopped. It was warm. I had to avoid the street where I lived. I struck north past the Cripplegate and turned along the London Wall. Only the poor were left. Fires had been lit at every street end. The air was thick with smoke. By the light of the flames I could see the dead-carts busy at work. Many victims lay in the streets where they had fallen. The Lord Mayor had banned funerals, but some still took place. With the screams, and the weeping, and the flames, and the fumes, I felt like I was in hell.

At last I came to London Bridge. I

was challenged by the Watch.

'You there! Come forward into the light!'

I had no wish to talk to the Watch, so I fled into a dark alley. My feet caught in something. I fell to the ground. I put out my hands to break my fall, and felt something soft. A corpse had tripped me up. I got up. The Watch turned into the alleyway, shouting for me to stop. I ran, straight into a door. There was no way out of the alley!

Then came a yell and a curse from behind me. The watchman had fallen over the corpse just as I had done. I ran towards him and jumped over both watchman and corpse. I ran off towards London Bridge. Once over, I would be well on my way. I could be at my uncle's farm by midday.

That was my hope. But armed men guarded the way on to the bridge. My journey was not going to be easy.

Chapter Six
A Fit of Madness

I later found that there was much less plague on the other side of the bridge. No one could cross the bridge at night. In the day you had to have a letter to say you didn't

have the disease. Otherwise you couldn't get past the guards. I was trapped north of the river. The great river flowed by. A fit of madness overtook me. I have always been a strong swimmer. But the Thames is very wide, and many have drowned in it. I wandered to the water's edge. There I found a great beam of wood. I might be able to swim across the river, using the beam to support me.

I took off my clothes and shoes. I bundled all my clothes up inside my jerkin and tied it to the beam of wood. I then cast the beam into the river, and jumped in beside it. I held

on to the beam and kicked with my
legs. Soon I was in the middle of the
river. The river was nearly at low
tide. Strong, dangerous currents
swept through the arches of London
Bridge. Instead of going to the
opposite bank, the current swept me
towards the bridge. I was in grave
danger.

My legs and arms were tiring fast.
Then a sudden twist of the current
tore my beam of wood away from
me. Under the water I went. I was
thrown this way and that. Any
moment I expected to be smashed
against the bridge. I was thrown

downwards, then up again. My head burst out of the water. At last I was able to take a breath.

I was east of the bridge. Not far away a boat was bobbing in the moonlight. I cried for help. Many would have ignored me. The good boatman pulled me aboard. I lay panting on the floor of the boat. And then came a bang. When I looked over, there was my beam. My clothes were still lashed to it.

My rescuer did not wish to keep me long in his boat. I might be infected with plague. He rowed me to the south bank, and left me there.

My luck had begun to turn. The Watch should have been there, but the bank was deserted. I pulled my wet clothes on. I was worn out and could do no more until daybreak. Not far from the river I found a house with a small garden. I lay on the soft grass beneath a tree.

When I woke, the sun was well up. An old woman screamed at me.

'Out! Out of my garden!'

A young girl came out of the house, rubbing her eyes. The old woman screamed at her too.

'Go indoors, Susan! He may have the plague! Tell your father to bring the dogs!'

I got to my feet, jumped over the low fence, and ran off into the countryside.

From here my journey should have been easy. I knew the way well. But people were wary of strangers from London. At Newington I met a gang of rough men. They blocked the road.

'Keep your distance!' roared one. 'Where are you from and what is your business?'

'I am from Camberwell. I walked

to Southwark yesterday on my uncle's business. Now I am returning home.'

The men were still suspicious.

'Did you cross into the city?'

'No.'

They still did not like the look of me. Then one of the other men spoke.

'I lived in Camberwell three years since. Who is this uncle of yours?'

'His name is John Peters. He is a farmer.'

The man nodded to the others.

'I know of John Peters. Let him pass.'

As I passed them, they moved well away from me, as if I were a leper. I was angry, but I knew they were right to be wary. They had wives and children, and were doing what they could to protect them.

I reached the turning to Camberwell. The sun was well up. I was hungry and thirsty. I drank from a stream by the road, but didn't feel any better. I had less than a mile to go, but the farm was too far away. The ache in my head got worse. I was dizzy. Many times I was sick in the road. If only I could rest somewhere cool. My brain was on fire. The fire spread to my arms and legs. A dark hedge looked cool and restful. I lay down under it. The pain got worse. I reached into my armpits and felt the swellings. I knew I had plague. I would die under this cool, dark hedge. I said a prayer for my mortal soul and closed my eyes for the last time.

Chapter Seven
The Return

A figure stood over me. I felt cool water at my lips. I tried to move. I tried to focus my eyes. I was so weak I could do neither. Then the figure went away, and I slept. When I

woke again, the figure was back.
This time, I could see who it was.
My brother, Jasper. I tried to speak,
but it was too hard. But I saw
another figure, and knew it to be my
mother. I wanted to weep for joy.

The days passed. I grew stronger.
At last my brother told me all that
had happened. I had almost reached
the farm without knowing it. My
brother found me. Not knowing I
had plague, he lifted me up and
carried me into the farm.

'We soon found the marks of
plague on you,' Jasper said. 'At first
our uncle was angry. But he is a

good man, and he agreed that you could stay in the barn. That was a week ago. Each morning, when we came to you, we thought we would find you dead. Then, three days ago, the buboes burst. The black poison left your body. That gave us hope. Since then, each day, you have got stronger.'

At last I was fully fit. I thanked my uncle for looking after my mother and brother, and for letting me stay.

'Stay until the plague has left the city,' my uncle said.

But I called my family together,

and told them I must return to London.

'Henry, the plague may have left you, but you are stark mad,' said Jasper. 'The plague is fiercer than ever in the city! Have you escaped once, only to catch it again?'

'Jasper, do you remember what Master Coulter said? Those who have once had the plague cannot catch it again. London holds no terrors for me. My place is with my master.'

I shook the hands of my uncle and brother, and kissed my mother and my aunt. Many tears were shed. I set off down the lane where I had lain down to die. Like that day, it was hot. But this time I was strong and well. I strode out on my journey. London Bridge, and the city that I loved, lay before me.

Author's note

Plague has caused millions of
deaths. The Great Plague of 1665
was the last great outbreak in
Britain. It caused over 100,000
deaths in London alone. The disease

can now be cured with antibiotics. In 1894, it was discovered that the disease is caused by a bacteria spread by fleas. It attacks the body in different ways. Bubonic plague causes painful black swellings on the body, as described in the story. Pneumonic plague is when the bacteria affects the lungs. This kind of plague is nearly always fatal. It may be the form of the disease that Henry's father died of. Septicaemic plague, which attacks the blood, is the most serious of all. It causes death within hours.

HUNTER'S MOON

John Townsend

Hunter's Moon

Thick smoke drifted across the moon. An owl flapped away into the blackness. Neil turned suddenly. He was sure the eyes were following his every move. Neil spun round in the mud. Then he ran off into the night.

When Neil was gone, the watcher returned. The fire was nearly out. The watcher kicked the embers into the damp grass, then stared up to greet the Hunter's Moon.

SHOUTING AT THE STARS

David Belbin

Shouting at the Stars

'Play *Open Book* again!'

Layla smiled. 'I'm glad you liked it,' she said.

'Play it again! All your other songs are rubbish!'

Layla didn't know what to say. She'd never had a heckler before.

'This is my last song,' she said.

'Good thing too!'

Layla got through the last song. But the day was ruined.

Tears of a Friend

Joanna Kenrick

Tears of a Friend

I am furious.

'What is my style? Looking boring? Being covered up? Wearing the cheap versions of your clothes? Oh, I know what my style is. It's to make you look better when you stand next to me. Thanks a lot!' I say. Claire's mouth hangs open.